THE AMULET
OF AVANTIA

BLAZE
THE
ICE DRAGON

With special thanks to Michael Ford

For Alex McAteer

www.beastquest.co.uk

ORCHARD BOOKS
338 Euston Road, London NW1 3BH
Orchard Books Australia
Level 17/207 Kent St, Sydney, NSW 2000

A Paperback Original
First published in Great Britain in 2009

Beast Quest is a registered trademark of Working Partners Limited
Series created by Working Partners Limited, London

Text © Working Partners Limited 2009
Cover illustrations by Steve Sims © Orchard Books 2009
Inside illustrations by Brian@KJA-artists.com © Orchard Books 2009

A CIP catalogue record for this book is available from
the British Library.

ISBN 978 1 40830 381 8

9 10 8

Printed in the UK by CPI Bookmarque, Croydon, CR0 4TD

The paper and board used in this paperback are natural recyclable
products made from wood grown in sustainable forests. The
manufacturing processes conform to the environmental regulations of
the country of origin.

Orchard Books is a division of Hachette Children's Books,
an Hachette UK company

www.hachette.co.uk

BLAZE
THE
ICE DRAGON

BY ADAM BLADE

ORCHARD BOOKS

The Forbidden Land

THE DEAD VALLEY

THE DEAD JUNGLE

THE DARKWOOD

THE DEAD PEAKS

All hail, fellow followers of the Quest.

We have not met before, but like you, I have been watching Tom's adventures with a close eye. Do you know who I am? Have you heard of Taladon the Swift, Master of the Beasts? I have returned – just in time for my son, Tom, to save me from a fate worse than death. The evil wizard, Malvel, has stolen something precious from me, and until Tom is able to complete another Quest, I cannot be returned to full life. I must wait between worlds, neither human nor ghost. I am half the man I once was and only Tom can return me to my former glory.

Will Tom have the strength of heart to help his father? This new Quest would test even the most determined hero. And there may be a heavy price for my son to pay if he defeats six more Beasts...

All I can do is hope – that Tom is successful and that I will one day be returned to full strength. Will you put your power behind Tom and wish him well? I know I can count on my son – can I count on you, too? Not a moment can be wasted. As this latest Quest unfolds, much rides upon it.

We must all be brave.

Taladon

PROLOGUE

Cries of pain drifted from the open door of the hut, but Derlot hurried on past towards the herb garden. He was one of the lucky ones – the terrible sickness had spared him so far. When the first shepherd had fallen sick from a hyena bite, no one in Rokwin had dreamt that the disease would spread. Derlot had been away at the market in Stonewin for two days, but by the time he returned the illness had touched almost every family in Rokwin. People were dying. Derlot just hoped that it was still in his power to help.

His father had been a medicine man, whose fame spread as far as the Plains. He'd claimed that one of his herbs, horn-fern, could cure any sickness in Avantia.

Derlot unlatched the gate to the herb garden and picked his way over the plants. Many of the herbs were withered and the weeds grew tall. But then he saw it – the horn-fern, its dark green leaves tipped with red.

Derlot stooped among the plants and took out his pruning knife. The blade was poised against the herb's stalk, when a howling sound cut through the still summer air. Was that more hyenas?

Derlot stood up and looked around. Something was coiling through the trees towards him – a strange, dark shape, like smoke trailing from a campfire. A sense of unease gripped him as he realised that it was moving too fast to be smoke.

Derlot felt his mouth drop open as his eyes told him something his mind refused to accept. The shape was some kind of dragon, but not the type described in children's tales. Green and red scales covered the creature's snake-like body. Its long tail swayed back and forth, and appeared to propel it through the air. The monster opened its icy jaws to reveal vicious fangs.

Derlot stumbled backwards towards the open garden gate, but tripped and landed on the path. The dragon hovered in the air above him, smoke coming from its nostrils. As it opened its mouth, Derlot threw his hands up to protect himself – he knew what was coming.

Fire.

But suddenly a blast of freezing air enveloped him. He lowered his hands and saw that the garden had changed. All the plants – including the precious horn-fern – were locked in ice. The ground at his feet was white with frost, and even the laces of his boots had frozen solid. The dragon had breathed ice.

The dragon hung lower in the sky, and Derlot was pinned by its gaze. There was something strange about its green eyes – something almost human. Was this a Beast or a man? Or some terrible mixture of the two?

With a shriek, the dragon whipped its tail onto the ground. The earth shook with the impact and the plants shattered like glass. Then the icy fragments became mist, blinding Derlot. As it cleared, he saw the dragon flying towards the volcano in Stonewin.

Derlot surveyed the ruins of the garden and gave a low wail of despair. Without his herbs, the villagers in Rokwin were doomed.

And as for the people of Stonewin, they had their own terrors to face.

CHAPTER ONE

LEAVING THE FORBIDDEN LAND

The sun was just a finger's breadth over the horizon as Tom and Elenna left the Dead Wood. Tom was tired. The battle with Luna the moon wolf had tested him to the limit – and Elenna, too.

"Perhaps we should rest," she suggested.

Tom glanced at his friend. Her

knees were scuffed from where she'd stumbled and fallen earlier. He then looked at their brave animal companions. Silver, Elenna's wolf, trotted on ahead with his head low, and Tom's horse, Storm, staunchly plodded forwards.

"I wish we could," Tom said regretfully. "But not yet."

He fingered the leather thong around his neck, from which hung the pieces of the Amulet of Avantia. So far he'd retrieved four amulet parts and defeated each of the Ghost Beasts that had guarded them. But his Quest would not be complete until he had all six pieces, and the amulet was whole again. Only then would he be able to bring his father, Taladon, back for good.

His next Quest, so his father had

told him, was to defeat a dragon called Blaze.

"Well, we need to stop and check the map," said Elenna. "We can drink some water at the same time."

Tom nodded and sat down on a boulder. Elenna took a flask from Storm's saddlebag and drank, while Tom stretched out his hand in front of him.

"Map!" he commanded.

The air rippled as the ghostly map appeared in front of him. Without this gift from Aduro, they would never have been able to find their way through the Forbidden Land or locate the Beasts.

The map showed a glowing line, like a thread of gold, snaking from where they stood at the edge of the Dead Wood, across the eastern fields, past a small village called Rokwin, and towards the town of Stonewin. It ended on the slopes of the volcano.

"Stonewin is where Epos lives," said Elenna, handing Tom the flask.

"I hope she's not in danger from this dragon," said Tom, taking a swig of water. Epos the flame bird was their loyal friend; on another occasion they had saved her from evil Wizard Malvel.

Tom placed a hand over his eyes and gazed in the direction of Stonewin. He called on the power to see across great distances given to him by the golden helmet, part of the suit of magical golden armour he had retrieved.

"There's the volcano at Stonewin," he said to Elenna. "But the crater isn't smoking. The volcano has

smoked since the day I was born. Something's wrong."

"Then let's not waste any more time," Elenna insisted.

Now Tom had seen their Quest set out on the ghost map, strength returned to his heart, and they sped towards Avantian soil. As if sensing his urgency, Storm and Silver seemed to find new reserves of energy.

But even though his determination to complete the Quest was as strong as granite, worry tugged at Tom's mind. Each time he defeated one of Malvel's Ghost Beasts, one of his golden armour powers vanished. Now he only had two left.

Tom shook his head. The people of Stonewin, and maybe even Epos herself, needed him. He would not let them down. He would not let Malvel win.

Tom and Elenna reached the high wall that separated the Forbidden Land from Avantia. They passed silently through the unmanned gate, back into familiarity.

"I'd forgotten that the sky could be so blue and the land so green," said Elenna. Storm whinnied and wheeled about, bolting off across the lush grass. Silver spun round in wild circles of joy.

"If we don't succeed in this Quest," said Tom, "Malvel's Beasts will take over Avantia, too – *everywhere* will be as dead looking as the Forbidden Land."

"We won't let that happen," said Elenna.

A fork of lightning suddenly split the sky, which had rapidly darkened.

"The Forbidden Land may be behind you," Malvel's voice rumbled thunderously above their heads, "but the curse of the Ghost Beasts is still strong. Four you have faced, but the Beast to come will be your end. No mortal can survive the dragon's breath."

"I do not fear Blaze!" shouted Tom.

Malvel laughed again. "Blaze will not be your only enemy this time. You will face two adversaries as one."

The storm ended as quickly as it had begun, and Malvel was gone.

"Two adversaries!" said Elenna. "What does he mean?"

"I don't know," said Tom grimly. "But I'm not afraid to find out."

CHAPTER TWO

A LAND OF ICE

Tom and Elenna mounted Storm and galloped across the Avantian Plain, Silver streaking beside them. Soon they were deep inside the kingdom, making good progress towards Stonewin.

Tom scanned the road ahead for danger, but to his surprise they saw no one at all. There weren't even any sheep grazing on the plains. Tom slowed Storm to a canter, and once they were on the grass, he vaulted off his horse and crouched to inspect the ground.

"There's frost on this grass!"

Elenna frowned. "But it's *summer*."

Tom shrugged and remounted Storm. They continued their journey, passing lush green fields and bushes heavy with berries. A short while later they came to a pond, and Tom guided Storm and Silver over to the water for a well-earned drink. But as they approached the edge, he saw that the surface was frozen over.

"This is no ordinary cold weather, Elenna," he said. "Some places are green and alive, while a few paces away the ground is frozen solid." Using the base of his shield, Tom smashed a hole in the ice so that

Storm and Silver could drink.

"How can that be?" said Elenna. "Stonewin's volcano has always made the surrounding areas warmer than usual, not colder."

They raced on. Soon, though, they came to a path that was covered with a great swathe of ice.

"We'll have to go slower," Tom told Elenna. "We can't risk injuring Storm on the slippery ground."

Picking their way carefully down the path, they passed a copse of trees bejewelled with frost and saw stone walls covered with ice.

Soon they came upon a signpost. One arm pointed towards Errinel, Tom's home village, and the other to Rokwin, which he knew was on the way to Stonewin.

"Let's hope we meet someone who can tell us what's going on," said Tom.

But he soon saw that the road towards Rokwin was deserted as well.

"People should be trading along this

route," said Elenna. "Where is everyone?"

Tom shared her bemusement. Even in the worst of weather the people of Avantia went about their business.

Tom heard a noise coming from ahead. Something was approaching from around the bend in the road. His hand fell to his sword hilt. Wild animals roamed Avantia, and he wouldn't be caught off guard. Elenna had already unhooked her bow.

"Ready?" she asked, fixing an arrow in place.

Tom nodded and held Storm's reins a bit tighter.

A mare trotted around the corner, steered by her rider, who lay close against her back.

Tom breathed a sigh of relief and

let go of his sword. "Stop there!
I need to talk to you."

But the horse didn't slow.

"Stop. Please!" Tom guided Storm
to stand sideways across the path.

The horse drew up in front of
them. Its rider was slumped in the
saddle, and only now turned his head
slowly towards them. Tom recoiled
when he saw the scabs covering the
man's face.

Silver let out a whine of unease.

"Are you all right?" Elenna asked the man.

"Go back," the sick man whispered. "Rokwin is doomed."

With those words, his eyes closed and he slipped from the saddle like a sack of grain. Tom could see that he was dead before he hit the ground. Silver took a few nervous steps towards the body, while Elenna got ready to dismount.

"No!" said Tom, guiding Storm between the man and the wolf.

"What's wrong?" said Elenna.

"For all we know, this man died of something contagious," Tom replied. "We mustn't touch him."

Tom steered along the edge of the path, as far as the bend in the road. There he dismounted and used his magical sight to look into the town of Rokwin. No smoke issued from the chimneys of the houses, and no one walked the streets.

A flash of movement caught his eye. Behind a large storehouse, a crowd of townspeople had gathered. But something was wrong. They walked in aimless circles, bumping into each other and falling over. Their faces were like the dead rider's – pale, with oozing sores. Some awful disease had infected the whole village.

With a troubled heart, Tom walked back to Elenna.

"What did you see?" she asked.

He told her the fate of the unfortunate villagers and she gasped. "What can we do for them?"

"First, we have to find whatever has caused this horror," said Tom. *And make sure the same thing doesn't happen to us*, he thought to himself. His Quest had just become twice as hard.

CHAPTER THREE

AMBUSHED

"Perhaps I can help them," said
Elenna. "My aunt taught me how
to use herbs as medicine."

Tom shook his head. "You can't,
Elenna. You might become infected
too."

"I'm not just leaving them, Tom,"
she replied hotly. "What about
Epos's talon?"

Tom looked at the golden talon

embedded in his shield, a reminder of his last visit to Stonewin, when he had freed the good Beast from Malvel's evil spell. The talon's healing powers had helped him many times, but this was different.

"The talon works on cuts and bruises," he explained. "The green jewel I took from Skor the winged stallion heals broken bones... But this is an illness – a *disease*. There's nothing we can do. We must focus on our Quest, and hope there's time to help afterwards."

Tom saw Elenna clench her fist with frustration. He put a hand on her shoulder and she ducked her head sadly.

"Is there another route to Stonewin?" she asked after a moment, her voice hoarse.

Tom summoned his map again, and studied its shimmering surface.

"We can skirt the lower reaches of Rokwin, instead of going directly through it," he said, pointing to a thin line on the map. "Behind the forest there."

They set off on their new route and found it was deserted as well. Soon Rokwin dipped out of sight behind a bank of tall trees. Elenna was quiet as they rode and Tom could tell that, like him, she felt guilty at leaving the suffering villagers behind.

The road gradually became rougher, the ground covered in loose rocks and hidden dips. Silver scouted the way, nose to the floor, guiding them onwards. But he stopped as he came to a felled tree that blocked the path.

Tom halted Storm.

"The locals must have been cutting down trees for timber," said Elenna. "The illness meant that they had to stop work."

"Or they blocked the road on purpose," said Tom.

The fallen trunk was as wide as he was tall. Skirting the fallen tree would be almost impossible, as the path was narrow and the land bordering them on either side was sheer and rocky.

"We'll have to turn back," said Elenna.

"We can't," Tom replied. "There's no other way to Stonewin." He patted Storm's neck. "What do you think, boy? Think you can clear that trunk?"

Storm tossed his mane, and stamped his front hooves. Tom knew

he could always rely on his horse's
bravery.

"Hold on tight," he said to Elenna,
and she gripped his waist.

Tom dug his heels into Storm's flank
and the stallion bolted forwards, his
hooves scattering rocks everywhere.
As the fallen trunk loomed, Tom lifted
the reins and gripped Storm's sides
with his knees. Suddenly they were
airborne and he felt his weight slam
back in the saddle.

Storm's hooves cleared the bark by
a finger's breadth, landing with a jolt
on the other side. "Well done!" cried
Tom, patting the horse's neck. He
looked back and saw Silver scramble
to the top of the trunk and stand
there, panting.

"Catch your breath, boy," Tom
called to the wolf. "You deserve—"

Something whizzed past Tom's ear – something fast and hot. He saw Silver spring away from the trunk and into the trees ahead.

"Take cover!" shouted Elenna.

Tom dragged Storm's reins around as a flare of light appeared between the trees ahead.

A flaming arrow.

The blazing shaft shot from the cover of the forest. In a moment, Tom's shield was on his arm and raised in defence. The arrow buried itself in his shield with a thud.

Then dozens of orange lights were visible in the forest, all illuminating angry faces.

Elenna sprang from Storm and Tom vaulted out of the saddle as well. He hit Storm's rear with his shield. "Go!" he shouted.

Storm bolted into the trees just as
a hail of flaming arrows descended.
Tom dragged Elenna behind him and
threw up his shield. The arrows
bounced off it.

The volley ended, but someone
shouted, "Fire again!"

Tom held up one hand, showing
the archers he was not a threat. "We
mean you no harm," he shouted.
"We're on a mission of peace."

41

Some muttering followed, and a voice called back, "Then turn around and go. You're not welcome here."

"We must get to Stonewin," Tom said. "The main road is filled with sickness."

"There's no sickness here, boy. We mean for it to stay that way."

Tom suddenly understood the reason behind their attack and took the risk of lowering his shield. A row of desperate faces looked back at him.

"This is our only option," said Tom. "Please…let us through. We're not sick."

One of the men stepped out of the trees, his bow down but the string taut with a loaded arrow. "Come forwards, then," he said. "Both of you."

Side by side, Tom and Elenna

cautiously drew within ten paces of the group. Tom felt his confidence returning. Now that he wasn't being shot at, he could reason with these people. Show them that he wasn't a threa—

The ground beneath him suddenly seemed to rise up, and Tom and Elenna were lifted off their feet and pulled into the air. They were caught in some sort of net hanging from a tree.

It was a trap.

Beside him, Elenna gave a scream of rage and fear and began to struggle against the net. Tom's eyes focused on the man below, who pointed his arrow straight up at them.

This time there was no escape.

CHAPTER FOUR

A VILLAGE
IN NEED

The bowman's hand – poised to
release the bowstring – shook with
nerves.

Tom struggled to right himself in
the net, but his legs kept slipping
through the gaps.

"Don't shoot," Tom implored. "Look
at us – we're not sick."

"We can't risk it," said a voice from
the woods. "Kill them."

"Very well," said the archer, holding the bow more firmly.

A scuffling sound came from the trees. Tom saw the man's eyes drop to his right and his mouth gape in surprise. Silver suddenly leapt from the shadows and sank his teeth into the man's arm. He screamed and dropped the bow and arrow.

Their enemy distracted, Tom managed to draw his sword and hack at the net.

"Hold onto me," he shouted to Elenna, and he felt her grip his waist. As the net fell open, he clutched one of the ropes with one hand, and the two friends swung out towards the archers, who were still among the trees. Tom let go and they dropped onto their enemies.

Elenna was up in a flash, her

hunting dagger at the throat of an elderly man. Tom rolled across the ground and pointed his sword at the chest of the injured archer. Silver came to stand at Tom's side.

"Lower your bows!" shouted Elenna, pressing the point of her knife against the old man's skin. Tom knew his friend would never harm an Avantian, but she was playing the role well.

He got to his feet, keeping his sword aimed at the injured archer. One by one, the flaming arrow-points were extinguished.

"Don't hurt him," said the elderly man. "He's only frightened, like the rest of us."

"We won't hurt anybody," said Tom. "We only want to talk."

Elenna released the man, who hobbled warily towards Tom. His eyes were dark from lack of sleep and his grey skin was like old parchment.

"My name is Derlot," he said. "I come from the village of Rokwin."

"I know the place," said Tom.

Derlot's face clouded. "You wouldn't recognise it now. Disease has ravaged it." He waved his hand at the faces between the trees. "We're the only ones who escaped."

The *clop-clop* of Storm's hooves made Tom turn. His stallion came out of the shelter of the woods and walked to his side.

"Where are you and your companions heading?" asked Derlot.

"Stonewin," said Tom, cautiously. "We are trying to reach the volcano there."

Derlot's eyes widened and he lowered his voice. "If the volcano is your destination, you must know of another threat to Avantia."

"What do you mean?" Tom asked.

Derlot stepped closer. "The plague is not the only curse to afflict this land. There's a dragon, too!"

Elenna looked at Tom in surprise, but Tom kept his face expressionless. Aduro had told him to never, ever reveal the truth of his Quests to anyone.

"A dragon!" he said. "Do they really exist?"

"I saw it with my own eyes," said Derlot. "A dragon that breathes ice instead of fire. My herbs to cure the ill were destroyed because of him."

Tom and Elenna shared a look. Did this explain the frozen ponds and icicles on the trees? Was Blaze responsible?

"If you don't believe me," said Derlot, "I can show you my herb garden. I just hope the dragon doesn't return."

Tom nodded. "Let's go."

Derlot guided them through the dense forest. Tom led Storm and Elenna followed with Silver at her side.

"No one in the village believes me," said Derlot, stooping under a branch. "But I know what I saw."

As they got deeper among the trees, slowly climbing the lower slopes of Rokwin, Tom noticed that the air was becoming colder.

Storm snorted and white clouds formed at his nostrils. Tom could see his own breath, too. They'd been travelling for some time, and Tom wondered if the old man was lost.

"Not far now," whispered Derlot, pulling his cloak more tightly around him.

They emerged into a clearing. Elenna gasped. Tom saw that the ground was white with frost and crystals of ice glittered like tiny diamonds on the tips of broken stalks and ruined shrubs.

"This was the herb garden," said Derlot, "and my only hope of curing the sickness that afflicts my people."

"Poor thing!" said Elenna, pointing to a rabbit among the ice-encrusted plants. It was frozen mid-jump, its ears sticking up and its body stretched out as it had tried to flee. This was surely more than just unseasonably cold weather.

Silver sniffed at the frozen rabbit, then turned his head to Elenna, as if confused that his prey was not running away.

"Do you believe me now?" asked Derlot. "About the dragon?"

Tom nodded, feeling a chill in his heart that had nothing to do with the freezing cold air. "I believe you," he said.

This time Malvel and his Beasts had gone too far.

CHAPTER FIVE

THE HYENAS OF ROKWIN

As they left the cold clearing behind, Elenna fell in step beside Derlot. "How was the sickness caused?" she asked.

"Five days ago," Derlot said, "one of the shepherds, Adam, was attacked and bitten by a hyena in the dark. He only managed to escape by beating the animal off with his staff and then climbing a tree."

Elenna held out her arm to help Derlot across a narrow stream.

"A hyena?" Tom exclaimed.

"Yes," Derlot continued. "It was strange because they don't normally come so close to Rokwin." The old man sighed. "Adam became sick in the night, sweating and mumbling in his sleep. By the next morning, the nurse looking after him was beginning to show signs of the same illness."

"It was spreading?" asked Tom, guiding Storm through a collection of boulders.

Derlot nodded. "The following dusk brought more hyenas. A dozen of them made a home in the thickets on the south side of the village. Their howls kept everyone awake. We posted archers and slingers around

Rokwin's fences, but under the full moon they attacked." Derlot shook his head mournfully. "They sneaked into houses and bit whoever they could find."

"Did they kill many people?" asked Elenna.

"That's the strange thing," said Derlot. "It was almost as though these hyenas hadn't come to kill. They would bite only once, and then slip away back to their den in the thickets. By the morning, half of the village was ill. Those who weren't decided to flee…"

This sounds like Malvel's magic, Tom thought. *Maybe the hyenas are the second adversary the Dark Wizard spoke of.*

When they reached the path again, it was almost dusk and the other villagers were waiting.

Elenna took Tom aside, while Derlot went to talk with his followers.

"Tom, we have to help these people," she whispered. "Even if it means delaying the Quest."

"You're right," he said. "I think Malvel is behind this, and we have to fight him wherever he appears. But what can we do about the plague?"

Elenna frowned for a moment, and then her face lit up. "My aunt always taught me that powdered willow bark was good for animal bites. Perhaps it'll work here, too."

"Do you have any?" Tom asked.

Elenna shook her head. "But the villagers may know where to find some."

She turned to the frightened group

and asked them if any willow trees grew nearby.

"Down by the river," replied a stout young woman. "It's a fair walk, but the trees are plentiful."

As Elenna gathered the villagers to head to the riverbank, Tom jumped onto Storm.

"Where are you going?" asked Derlot.

"To deal with the hyenas," said Tom. "They're on the south side of the village, you say?"

"Yes," said Derlot, "but there are many. A boy like you will be torn to pieces."

Tom smiled. "I've faced hyenas before. They don't frighten me." He saw that Elenna was ready to go. "Be careful," Tom warned her. "There may be hyenas by the river, too."

Elenna crouched beside her wolf. "I have Silver to look after me." She stroked the thick hair behind his neck. "You're not scared of a few mangy hyenas, are you?"

Silver growled and bared his teeth. Tom felt much better knowing that the wolf was at his friend's side.

He spurred Storm into action and galloped off along the road towards Rokwin.

Night was falling and every sound was magnified in Tom's ears. On either side the forest pressed down upon him. Owls seemed to hoot in welcome as he passed the outskirts of the village of Rokwin.

Soon the road disappeared, and Tom found himself surrounded by thorny bushes. *This must be the thicket Derlot meant,* he thought. Storm slowed, tossing his head with a whinny. Tom stroked the horse's mane and slipped off his back. There were tracks on the ground made by large pawprints – hyenas.

Low growls came from the thicket.

"Stay here," Tom whispered to Storm, and set off in a crouch, following the sound. The sinister laughter of hyenas drifted over the night air as Tom crept between the sharp thorny branches. Then he saw them.

A pack of mangy creatures, their ribs showing through their hides, were fighting in a clearing. Grass and dust flew up as they tore at each other with their teeth and claws. Saliva drooled from their jaws, and

they howled and gnashed their teeth.
Tom counted them: ten altogether.
He would have to form a plan so he
could fight them all at once.

Tom felt his nose twitch. A rank
smell, like rotten meat, had filled his
nostrils. Then he heard a tiny shuffle
nearby. Tom twisted, drawing his
sword just in time as a snarling hyena
leapt from behind him. He thrust his
sword towards the animal and it died

on his blade. With his foot, Tom pushed the dead creature off his weapon.

The growls from the clearing had stopped. Tom looked up.

Ten pairs of eyes were on him, like twenty silver coins glittering in the moonlight. One by one, the hyenas loped forwards.

Then they broke into a run, coming straight for Tom. There was death in their eyes.

CHAPTER SIX

A NIGHT ATTACK

Tom knew he couldn't face all the hyenas at once, and he sprinted back towards Storm. He no longer had the ability from the golden armour to jump great distances, so he threw himself onto Storm's saddle. The hyenas surrounded him.

"Go!" he yelled, kicking his stallion's sides. Storm charged straight through the hyenas, causing them to scatter.

One yelped as it was trampled beneath the stallion's hooves.

The other hyenas regrouped and howled into the night, flashing their long yellow fangs.

A plan formed in Tom's head, but he'd have to make the hyenas follow him for it to work. Storm reared on his hind legs in alarm as the scavenging animals came closer, but Tom calmed him down.

"It's all right, boy," he said. "We're going to get out of this."

The hyenas paced back and forth, arching their spines, the hair on their necks standing straight up.

Again, Tom rode Storm directly at the mangy creatures. One leapt up, but he swiped at it with the flat of his sword. The others dodged aside, their thin black lips curled into snarls.

Tom galloped back along the road, past Rokwin and through the forest. Behind him he could hear the yapping of the hyenas as they pursued him. They were close. Storm charged between the trees fearlessly, the branches whipping at Tom's face.

A bank of solid trunks blocked the path and Tom changed direction. Two hyenas moved quickly through the undergrowth and threw themselves at Storm's flank. Tom let go of the reins to beat one away with his shield, stabbing at the other.

Storm burst through the far side of the forest. They were out in the fields again, heading back towards the Forbidden Land. Storm was soaked with sweat, and his mane streamed in the darkness, but he galloped on.

When it seemed they were pulling away from the hyenas, Tom slowed his horse down to keep their pursuers in the chase. He couldn't afford to lose them now. Not when his plan was nearly complete.

They passed the frozen pond where he and Elenna had re-entered Avantia and then plunged back into the Dead Wood. It had been the location of his previous Quest, against Luna the moon wolf, and Tom steered Storm along the complicated paths that led between the trees. It was as if they'd been etched into his brain. The yellow jewel he won defeating Narga the sea monster had given him a perfect memory.

As they threaded between the bare silvered trunks, the padding of the hyenas' paws behind them grew softer. Tom risked a look back, and saw only four or five of the creatures slinking through the shadows. They looked uncertain. His ruse had worked: the hyenas were disorientated and in unfamiliar territory. And several of them were already lost in the forest.

Tom's legs ached from gripping Storm's flanks, but he did not slacken his hold. He criss-crossed the woods until the last of the hyenas fell to the ground, its tongue lolling from its exhausted mouth. Then Tom galloped away, leaving it deep in the maze of dark trees. With any luck, none of the hyenas would return to spread disease ever again.

It was the middle of the night when Tom and Storm trotted back down the forest path towards Rokwin. Grey smoke curled into the sky from the small fires that lit the outskirts of the village. The uninfected villagers he'd seen in the forest were huddled at the firesides, boiling a foul-smelling broth in iron pots. Tom found Elenna beside one. Silver lay patiently at her feet.

"You're back!" she said.

Tom slipped from Storm's back. "The hyenas will no longer be a problem."

"We've been busy here as well. We found the willow bark," Elenna said, and they walked to where two thin and bedraggled women were sleeping soundly. Another was sitting up, sipping from a wooden cup.

"These three women were sick only a few hours ago."

Tom smiled through his weariness.

"Your friend is very skilled," said a voice he recognised. Tom saw Derlot coming towards them. "We've enough medicine to heal everyone. Soon the whole of Rokwin will be cured."

Tom was happy, but he couldn't allow himself to relax. One obstacle was overcome, but Malvel's Beast still awaited them.

"We should go," he said.

"No!" exclaimed Derlot. "We must give you a feast. You have both saved our lives."

"I'm afraid we have another problem to deal with," said Tom. "And it cannot wait."

"The dragon?" Derlot whispered.

Tom nodded, unable to lie. He climbed onto Storm, and helped Elenna up behind him. "Goodbye, Derlot," he said.

"Farewell, young heroes," the old man replied. The villagers cheered and waved them off, shouting their thanks.

Storm galloped along the rocky path towards Stonewin, Silver at his side, and soon the crackle of the villagers' fires and the smell of wood-smoke were far behind.

When he saw the volcano rise up ahead in the distance, Tom felt as though he was returning home. He smiled to himself as he remembered the last time he had visited this place – on his Quest to free Epos. Back then, the sight of the gigantic flame bird with her blazing feathers had filled him with dread. But once rescued from Malvel's spell, Epos had become one of his most loyal friends.

Tom frowned. The volcano had lost its bitter smell of sulphur and the air wasn't as warm as it should have been. It was as if the great volcano had become dormant and sapped of life.

Using his magical sight, Tom scoured the slopes for Malvel's fifth Ghost Beast. Nothing stirred in the darkness. "We should stop for the night," he said. "We can look for Blaze when the sun rises."

Elenna seemed happy to rest, and lay with Silver in the shelter of a large boulder. Storm lounged by the side of the path and Tom sat against his soft underbelly, determined to keep his eyes open in case danger approached.

His mind returned to Epos. Was the flame bird in danger? If Malvel had

harmed her, Tom vowed that
his revenge would be swift. But his
anger didn't keep him awake. The
stars began to drift in front of his
eyes, and he felt sleep envelop him.

He woke with a start. An icy feeling
pressed against his chest.

Tom looked down and saw
something moving across his torso.
His hands touched the green and red
scales, thick as saddle leather, which
coiled around him.

Blaze!

CHAPTER SEVEN

A FAMILIAR FOE

Panic and pain choked Tom's throat as the dragon's length tightened around him. He tried to stand up, but he couldn't move his legs. The dragon had looped its snaky form around his lower body. Two gleaming eyes set in a narrow head on a long neck swung round to look straight at him.

Tom stared as a forked tongue, black as night, flickered in and out between the Beast's bloodless reptilian lips. The dragon brought its head right up to Tom's face. Tom wanted to look away, but he couldn't. There was something about the dragon's eyes. They weren't like any Beast's he'd seen before. They looked…human. Tom was sure he'd seen them somewhere before.

He tried to call out to Elenna, but a thin wheezing sound was the only noise that came from his mouth. He writhed, attempting to push out his arms. He twisted his shoulders and jerked his hips – anything to loosen the dragon's death-hold. As if in response, the scaly body contracted and Tom felt his ribs begin to crack.

Storm snorted in the darkness and

Elenna slept on, a few paces away from Tom and oblivious to the danger. He had to wake her. If he died, she would be next. Tom saw his shield leaning up against a rock. If he could knock it over the sound might awaken Elenna.

As the Beast's muscular grip shifted again, Tom gasped as he tried to draw breath. The ice dragon's head didn't move – it was as if Blaze wanted to *watch* him suffocate. Then Tom realised where he had seen those eyes before.

Malvel!

Somehow the Dark Wizard was *inside* the Beast, controlling him with his evil magic.

With a mighty effort, Tom stretched his leg towards the shield, managing to slip his foot behind it. Summoning

the last vestiges of his strength, he
flicked the shield up into the air and
it clattered onto a small rock.

Elenna was on her feet in a
heartbeat.

Tom's vision darkened and his limbs
grew weak. Was this the end?

Suddenly Blaze's death-grip
weakened and air filled Tom's lungs.
He immediately saw the cause. One
of Elenna's arrows was sticking out
from the dragon's body. Silver
charged forwards and tried to bite
Blaze's side, but his teeth slid
helplessly off the thick scales.

"Hold on!" Elenna shouted,
stringing another arrow to her bow.
Tom wriggled free and rolled across
the ground towards his sword. But
before he could grab the hilt, the
tentacle-like coil of Blaze's tail

wrapped around his ankle. Tom
looked over his shoulder and saw
that he was being dragged towards
the Beast's gaping jaws. The dragon's
teeth were a chilly green, but his
mouth was blood-red.

Tom pulled himself by his
fingernails towards the sword, feeling
his sinews stretch to their limit.

Finally, he locked his fingers around the hilt. As he was pulled backwards, he turned and swiped at the Beast's head. But the blade passed straight through the dragon and thwacked into the ground. Blaze's body was now see-through. He'd turned into a ghost!

Tom felt himself swell with rage as he got to his feet. Like the other Beasts on this Quest, Blaze had the ability to transform from a real to a ghostly form in an instant. Tom swung with his sword again, trying to hack at the semi-transparent scales, but once more his sword met no resistance and passed through the Beast. The colour rushed back into Blaze's body as he took on his flesh-and-blood form.

"Look!" shouted Elenna, pointing.

"The amulet piece!"

Tom's heart thumped as he saw that the amulet fragment was lodged between the scales where Blaze's body met his head. Tom hopped onto a boulder and leapt towards the dragon, reaching for his prize.

The Beast lashed its tail out like a whip and Tom was struck in the chest and fell to the ground. He watched helplessly as the ice dragon took to the skies, climbing steadily through the air, his tail whipping out behind to thrust him upwards. Silver howled at the departing Beast while Storm neighed angrily.

Blaze hovered above the volcano's crater and Malvel's laughter boomed, shaking the slopes. "Come and catch me…if you dare." With those words, Blaze dipped his head and plunged into the heart of the crater.

Tom got to his feet.

"It sounds like a trap," said Elenna.

The first pale light of dawn was breaking. Tom realised they hadn't slept for long, but he wasn't tired. Coming so close to death had made him feel more alive than ever.

"We've outsmarted Malvel before – we'll outsmart him again! We must go after Blaze."

Tom saw Storm's legs twitch, as if the horse was eager to start the day.

"You stay here, boy," said Tom. "We should travel by foot on the volcano."

Elenna stroked Silver. "And you look after him," she said.

Waving goodbye to their animal companions, Tom and Elenna set off up the path. The cold air cut right through them.

"Do you remember the last time we were here?" asked Elenna, as they climbed up the craggy rock face. "Lava flowed down from the crater edge."

Tom nodded as he scrambled onto a ledge. "The villagers would have lost their homes, but we succeeded in our Quest and saved Epos."

"Epos…" said Elenna, her voice grave. "Where is she? Why is it so cold up here?

Tom looked up towards the crater, where Epos's nest was. So far he hadn't even felt her presence. His anger tightened like a knot inside him. "If Malvel has harmed my friend," he said, "he will pay."

CHAPTER EIGHT

EPOS IMPRISONED

The air grew even colder as they climbed up the winding path of the barren slopes. It was as though all the laws of nature had been turned upside down.

As they headed towards the crater's edge, the shrieking wind stung Tom's eyes and carried his breath away on icy currents. He looked over at Elenna, and saw that her lips had started to turn purple.

"Are you all right to go on?" he shouted above the wind.

"W-w-while I c-c-c-can still fire an arrow, I won't stop," she called back.

Pain throbbed in Tom's legs as he picked his way over the final yards to the edge of the crater. Long ago he'd watched Epos majestically rise from this very spot, her ruby-red feathers aflame and her talons dipped in gold. Where was she now?

Elenna reached his side, the wind lashing her hair across her pale face. They both peered into the chasm below.

Tom's heart filled with despair. The shallow sides of the crater were covered in crystals of ice. Great blue-white columns rose up from the depths like towers of diamonds. The lava pool itself, which should have been bubbling at the bottom of the crater, was completely frozen over with a sheet of solid ice. And there, below the surface, was a sight that made Tom more despairing still. Epos, her mighty wings spread wide, was trapped under the ice shelf!

"Poor Epos!" gasped Elenna. "Only Malvel could be so cruel."

Tom was almost speechless with anger. "We have to rescue her!"

Blaze was nowhere to be seen, so they began to climb down the steep walls of the crater, placing each foot with care. Epos glided up to the roof of her frozen prison. A fireball like a miniature sun formed between her talons, and she hurled it against the ice shelf.

"She's trying to escape," said Elenna.

Epos did the same again, and this time Tom saw a crack appear in the frozen sheet. They reached the flatter ground by the frozen lava pool and watched as another of the flame bird's fiery orbs hit the ice, causing a second fissure to appear in the ice shelf.

"It's working," said Elenna.

"One more, Epos!" Tom urged. "You can do it!"

As the fourth fireball was growing between the flame bird's talons, a roar from above shook the walls of the volcano. Tom looked up. Blaze was diving towards them, his mouth open wide, razor teeth dripping with drool, and his human eyes glinting with ferocious intent. Malvel's cackle echoed around the crater.

The Beast swooped past them, a surge of icy air blasting from his jaws,

which he directed over the ice shelf.
Tom felt his heart sink – the frozen
sheet was now twice as thick.

Epos's fireballs were having little
effect on the toughened barrier, but
still she tried, hurling ball after ball

against the ice. Each time it looked as if her efforts might succeed, the Beast blew more freezing air to cut off her escape. Blaze seemed only interested in keeping Epos imprisoned and paid no attention to Tom and Elenna.

"There must be a way to stop Blaze," said Elenna.

"We don't have to stop him," said Tom. "We just have to keep him busy and give Epos a chance to escape. Can you distract him long enough for me to get down to the ice shelf?"

Elenna had strung an arrow before the words were out of his mouth.

"Good," he said. "Get Blaze's attention."

Elenna loosed an arrow across the cavern at the dragon and Blaze shrieked in pain as it found its mark in his side. Tom began scrambling down to the ice, sliding over the slippery ground. He saw Elenna fire another arrow, but this time Blaze shifted into his ghost form and it passed straight through him.

Tom was now down on the ice. Seeing him so close, Epos hurled another fireball at the shelf.

"Look out!" Tom heard Elenna call. He turned to see Blaze flying right at him. He dived aside as a blast of ice shot from the dragon's mouth. Tom sprang up and lunged at the Beast. He swung his sword as the dragon wheeled in the air, but at the last instant Blaze became a ghost and the blade passed through him. With another freezing blast, the dragon had reinforced the ice shelf.

How can I defeat this Beast? Tom wondered. *I can't even get near him!*

Undaunted, Epos lit another ball, the bright light shining through the ice and casting Tom's shadow onto the volcano's wall. Tom saw Blaze coming at him again and he sprang up, trying to drive the point of his sword into the Beast's heart. Once more, Blaze assumed his ghostly form and the attack was in vain. The evil Beast hovered, semi-transparent, just above Tom's head.

"Out of tricks?" Malvel's voice sneered.

Tom's anger took over, and he slashed his sword wildly at the air.

Out of the corner of his eye, Tom saw his shadow make the same movement, and to his surprise Blaze shrieked and writhed. It was as though the blade of Tom's shadow had somehow connected with the

Ghost Beast. A fat drop of blue blood dripped from Blaze's scales.

Tom's eyes were drawn to Epos. For some reason the flame bird was clutching a fireball, but hadn't thrown it. The light from the fireball meant that Tom cast a looming shadow on the wall. *Could it be…?* Yes, Epos was telling him something important.

Tom stabbed wildly again, and his shadow's blade connected with the Ghost Beast. Blaze roared with pain for a second time, confusion showing in his glinting eyes. But Tom wasn't confused – he now understood why Epos was holding the fireball. It made Tom's shadow permanent. His skin tingled as he realised what this meant.

I might not be able to fight the Ghost Beast, he thought, *but my shadow can!*

CHAPTER NINE

SHADOW WARRIOR

Tom readied himself to strike again, but the Ghost Beast surged upwards, landing on an icy ledge out of the reach of Tom's shadow. Tom knew that he had to press his advantage while the Beast was stunned with his injuries, but how could he attack Blaze with his shadow while the Ghost Beast cowered far above him?

Of course, he thought. *The white jewel!* He pulled the gem he had won from Kaymon the gorgon hound out of his belt. It gave him the power to separate himself from his shadow.

Tom climbed up to Elenna, who kept her bow trained on the ice dragon in case he shifted out of his ghostly form. He whispered in her ear so that Malvel wouldn't be able to hear his plan.

"My shadow is the only thing that can harm Blaze while he is in his ghost form," he said. "And the only way my shadow can reach him is if I use the jewel from Kaymon."

Elenna frowned. "It's too dangerous, Tom," she whispered back. "When your shadow is separated from you, your body can't move. You won't be able to defend yourself if Blaze comes after you."

Tom could see that she spoke out of worry for him, but he would not be swayed. "I know it's a risk," he said, "but if we wait here, Blaze will recover, and he'll freeze us just like that rabbit in Derlot's garden."

Suddenly Epos gave a tired-sounding cry and the fireball in her talons faded a little. Tom looked back at Elenna, whose face had hardened.

"I'll do my best to protect you," Elenna said. "If Blaze comes too close, I'll have my arrows ready."

Tom gave Elenna a quick hug of thanks, then took a deep breath, calling on the power of the white jewel.

Dizziness gripped his head, and he put out a foot to steady himself before he opened his eyes.

But he hadn't moved.

"Tom," said Elenna excitedly. "It's working!"

One leg of his shadow had peeled away. Tom ordered the other leg to do the same, and his shadow stood beside him as though it were a whole other person. In his mind, Tom told it to unsheathe its sword. Though his own arms were as still as a statue, his shadow drew its blade.

Do battle with Blaze, he told it. Tom was powerless to move, but his shadow did exactly as he asked, darting across the ice and clambering up the far side of the cavern wall towards the ledge where Blaze was beginning to stir once again.

Quicker! Tom urged. His shadow rippled silently over the wall, and heaved itself onto the ledge.

The Ghost Beast immediately turned to face the shadow, striking out with his tail. The shadow ducked and countered with its blade, bringing out a bloodcurdling cry of agony from the ice dragon. Blaze leapt off the ledge and glided downwards, blowing another fresh layer of ice onto Epos's prison. Tom's shadow jumped down too, its sword held aloft, relentlessly chasing Blaze.

Why didn't Malvel's Beast stay and fight? Tom wondered. *Why was it so important to keep the ice shelf in place?*

Epos, looking re-energised, lit another fireball, while Blaze and Tom's shadow faced off again. The Ghost Beast darted forwards, dodged the shadow's sword at the last moment, then flicked his muscular tail out. It struck Tom's shadow in the head, knocking him back against the wall. Tom felt the bruising pain as though his actual body had been hit.

But instead of going after the shadow, Blaze breathed another icy blast at Epos, refreezing the ice shelf.

Realisation dawned in Tom's mind. Blaze was an *ice dragon*. Epos was a *flame bird*. Just as ice could imprison Epos, what if *heat* was Blaze's enemy? Was that why Blaze was keeping Epos imprisoned?

Tom wished he could tell Elenna his theory. She might be able to help Epos break the ice and escape. But his voice, like the rest of him, was paralysed. No, he would have to handle this on his own.

Somehow, he would have to move.

His brain told him it was impossible, but his heart told him otherwise.

Tom sent his shadow running to the far side of the cavern, and Blaze followed. While they were busy, Tom channelled all his willpower into making his frozen limbs move. He felt a sweat break out all over his body, and his heart thundered in his chest. He managed to make his head turn, but it felt as though the sinews in his neck were being torn apart. Next he concentrated on moving his arm. It was like trying to lift the anvil in his uncle's forge. His body screamed with pain, but the arm finally moved a fraction. His eyes caught Elenna's expression – her mouth was wide open in amazement.

It took all his strength of heart, but somehow Tom dragged his body over to Epos's ice prison. He lifted his shield above his head. Beneath the ice, Epos flapped her wings madly in anticipation. The sight was enough to drive Tom on. With a growl of determination, he brought the shield down, ramming it into the ice.

A crack splintered the centre of the sheet and Tom fell to his knees. He watched with delight as Epos burst free in a shower of icy splinters and took to the air. The crater was suddenly filled with golden light and, all around, the ice began to melt and trickle in rivulets down the walls.

Malvel's cry of despair split the cavern, and Blaze suddenly became his solid form once again. Through the searing heat, the Beast's green and red scales glistened. It seemed Blaze couldn't remain a ghost in the midst of the smoking molten rock. The dragon hovered over Tom's shadow, but the solid Beast posed it no danger.

"You've done it!" cried Elenna. "Epos is free."

Despite this, Tom knew the Quest was far from over. He still couldn't move properly, and was vulnerable until his shadow returned to him. He knelt on the remains of the ice and called his shadow back.

But Blaze had already spotted him. The dragon turned its massive body and began flying in for the attack.

Tom's shadow ran behind, but it wasn't as quick as the Beast.

As Blaze slithered through the air towards him, Tom again saw the amulet piece near the dragon's shoulder – the amulet piece he needed to bring his father back to his flesh and blood form. Now he feared that would never happen. The icy jaws gaped, ready to devour him.

CHAPTER TEN

FACE TO FACE WITH MALVEL

Elenna's arrow thudded into Blaze's neck and the Beast veered off-course, smashing into the ground. The distraction gave Tom's shadow enough time to return to his body.

As Tom joined up with his shadow once more, power surged through him. He sprang to his feet. "Thanks, Elenna!" he called.

"Now finish off that Beast!" she yelled back.

"With pleasure," Tom muttered, seeing Blaze rise up. He couldn't use his ghostly form to escape any more.

Blaze's green eyes flashed. "You'll die in this volcano, Tom," said a voice. It was a roar, but the tone was Malvel's.

The dragon sent a jet of freezing air towards Tom. He threw himself out of the way, feeling the icy air brush his legs.

Epos swooped down and crashed into Blaze, her talons raking his skin. Tom saw something drop to the ground and land in the corner of the volcano, next to a bubbling chasm of lava.

The amulet fragment!

"Get the amulet piece!" Tom

shouted to Elenna, as Blaze shook
Epos loose and faced him again. The
dragon released another jet of ice and
Tom charged forwards, ducking
beneath the icy stream and stabbing
upwards with his sword. The blade
lodged in the thick scales of the
dragon's stomach and Tom lost his
grip on the hilt as Blaze soared up
into the air.

Looking over, Tom saw Elenna slip the precious amulet fragment inside her pocket, and he ran to her side.

Blaze whipped around to face them and stalked forwards, Tom's sword still hanging from his underside. Tom and Elenna found themselves right by the edge of a molten pool. There was nowhere they could go.

Epos cawed from above and descended to attack Blaze, but the dragon flicked his tail out and sent the flame bird spinning into the lava.

"I told you that you'd die here," screeched Malvel's voice.

Blaze arched his back and readied himself to deliver the final attack. But instead of fear, Tom felt a strange calm. There was a way out of this predicament. He just had to outwit both the Beast and the Dark Wizard.

Tom took a few steps forward.

"What are you doing?" shouted Elenna. "You'll get yourself killed!"

"Stay back," said Tom. If Elenna was too close, his plan would fail.

White smoke appeared in Blaze's nostrils and the dragon opened his mouth to release his icy breath. Tom waited until the last possible moment, then lifted his shield as the blast shot forth. The freezing air hammered into it. Peering over the rim, Tom saw the flow of ice rebounding off the shield's surface and deflecting back at Blaze, encasing him in ice. Tom held on, even as the wood of his shield started to creak. The air around him was bitterly cold, but Nanook's bell, which he had won when he freed the snow monster, protected him. Slowly, a thick icy

barrier appeared between Tom and
Blaze, reaching all the way out to the
edge of the volcano's wall.

Tom checked behind him, and saw
Elenna shivering with the cold. Her
teeth were chattering, but she
managed a smile. Tom was glad she'd
stayed back; any closer, and her
blood would have frozen.

Then she held a shaky arm out, and pointed past him. "M...M...Malvel," she stuttered.

Tom turned back and saw the Dark Wizard lying on the ground beside the frozen Beast. The cold must have driven him out of the dragon's body. He climbed to his feet, shaking his head in confusion, before catching sight of Tom through the ice wall. He stepped forwards and ran his fingers over the cold surface, his eyes never leaving Tom's.

"Blaze is finished," Tom told Malvel. "And so are you."

The Dark Wizard smashed his fists against the wall.

"This isn't over!" he screamed. "I'll have my revenge!"

Tom ran at the wall, hoping to crash through it. A thin crack appeared. He wanted nothing more than to face his archenemy one-on-one.

But Malvel's mouth curled to a smirk, and he slowly backed away. "Another time, young adversary," he said. "Another time."

"While there's blood in my veins," shouted Tom, ramming the ice with his shoulder again, "I'll defeat you!"

Malvel's form seemed to drift out of the volcano wall, and Blaze faded away with him. The sword that had been lodged in the dragon's belly clattered to the ground.

Epos appeared by their side, her wings blazing with healthy flames. A fireball hovered between her talons. Tom stepped back as the flame bird sent it spinning into the ice wall.

As the fire died, a hole appeared

in the centre of the wall, melting outwards. When it was big enough, Tom and Elenna climbed through.

Tom knelt and picked up his sword. "Malvel was so close to us," he said. "Almost close enough to touch."

"Don't worry, Tom," Elenna said. "At least we have this." She held up the amulet piece.

Tom took the fragment and joined it with the others that hung around his neck. As soon as he did so a light appeared before them, almost blinding in its brightness. And there, only a few paces away, was a ghostly shape he knew as well as his own reflection.

"Father!" Tom cried.

"You have triumphed once more, my son," said Taladon. "Epos is safe, and Malvel is driven back for now."

Tom longed to throw his arms around his father, but he knew it was impossible. Until he collected the sixth and final piece of the amulet, his father would remain a ghost.

"We only have one more Quest to go," said Tom. "Then you'll be flesh and blood again."

Taladon nodded slowly. "One last Quest, but a Quest deadlier than all those that have come before. Hold fast to your courage. You will need it."

With those words, he disappeared.

Tom longed to keep his father with him, but put his sadness from his mind.

On the other side of the ice wall, Epos spread her wings. "I think she's offering us a ride," said Elenna.

Tom climbed onto the flame bird's back, and Elenna settled beside him.

The Beast leapt into the air, beat her
wings, and took them up through the
glowing crater. When they emerged
into the clear air of Avantia, Tom
heaved a sigh of relief. The frost from
the land had gone.

They dismounted Epos on
Stonewin's peak, and the flame bird
dived back into the volcano.

Tom was pleased that he'd succeeded in his Quest, but he knew that Malvel's sorcery would not be kept at bay for long. And there was a sixth and final Beast to face.

"The end is close," Elenna said.

"One last push," he replied. *And I'll be ready when you come again, Malvel,* Tom thought. *I'll always be ready.*

Win an exclusive
Beast Quest T-shirt and goody bag!

In every Beast Quest book the Beast Quest logo is hidden
in one of the pictures. Find the logos in books 19 to 24
and make a note of which pages they appear on.
Send the six page numbers in to us.
Each month we will draw one winner to receive
a Beast Quest T-shirt and goody bag.

Send your entry on a postcard listing
the title of this book and the winning
page number to:

THE BEAST QUEST COMPETITION:
THE AMULET OF AVANTIA
Orchard Books
338 Euston Road, London NW1 3BH
Australian readers should email:
childrens.books@hachette.com.au

New Zealand readers should write to:
Beast Quest Competition
4 Whetu Place, Mairangi Bay, Auckland, NZ
or email: childrensbooks@hachette.co.nz

Only one entry per child.
Final draw: 31 May 2010

You can also enter this competition
via the Beast Quest website: www.beastquest.co.uk

Fight the Beasts,
Fear the Magic

www.beastquest.co.uk

Have you checked out the all-new Beast Quest website?
It's the place to go for games, downloads, activities,
sneak previews and lots of fun!

You can read all about your favourite Beast Quest
monsters, download free screensavers and desktop
wallpapers for your computer, and send
beastly e-cards to your friends.

Sign up to the newsletter at www.beastquest.co.uk
to receive exclusive extra content and the opportunity
to enter special members-only competitions. It's the best
place to go for up-to-date info on all the Beast Quest
books, including the next exciting series,
which features six brand new Beasts.

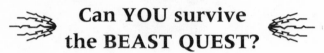

Can YOU survive the BEAST QUEST?

Read all of Tom's incredible adventures as he battles the fearsome Beasts sent by evil Wizard Malvel. Together with his loyal friend Elenna, his trusty steed Storm and Silver the grey wolf, Tom risks everything in his fight for the freedom of Avantia.

Will good conquer evil? Or will Malvel and his Beasts destroy the kingdom? As long as there is blood in his veins, Tom is determined to stop him…

Do BATTLE with your friends!

Each exciting story comes with FREE collector cards! Cut them out and play with your friends. Keep an eye out for a special exclusive collector card – check the Beast Quest website for details.

www.beastquest.co.uk

FREE COLLECTOR CARDS INSIDE!

Series 1

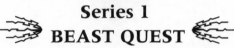

BEAST QUEST

An evil wizard has enchanted the Beasts that guard Avantia. Is Tom the hero who can free them?

978 1 84616 483 5   978 1 84616 482 8   978 1 84616 484 2

978 1 84616 486 6   978 1 84616 485 9   978 1 84616 487 3

Can Tom save the baby dragons from Malvel's evil plans?

978 1 84616 951 9

FREE COLLECTOR CARDS INSIDE!

Series 2
THE GOLDEN ARMOUR

Tom must find the pieces of the magical golden armour.
But they are guarded by six terrifying Beasts!

ZEPHA
978 1 84616 988 5

CLAW
978 1 84616 989 2

SOLTRA
THE STONE CHARMER
978 1 84616 990 8

VIPERO
978 1 84616 991 5

ARACHNID
THE KING OF SPIDERS
978 1 84616 992 2

TRILLION
THE THREE-HEADED LION
978 1 84616 993 9

SPECIAL BUMPER EDITION!

Will Tom find Spiros
in time to save his
aunt and uncle?

SPIROS
THE GHOST PHOENIX
978 1 84616 994 6

FREE COLLECTOR CARDS INSIDE!

Series 3
 THE DARK REALM

To rescue the good Beasts, Tom must brave the terrifying Dark Realm and six terrible new Beasts...

TORGOR
THE MINOTAUR

978 1 84616 997 7

SKOR
THE WINGED STALLION

978 1 84616 998 4

NARGA
THE SEA MONSTER

978 1 40830 000 8

KAYMON
THE GORGON HOUND

978 1 40830 001 5

TUSK
THE MIGHTY MAMMOTH

978 1 40830 002 2

STING
THE SCORPION MAN

978 1 40830 003 9

SPECIAL BUMPER EDITION!

ARAX

978 1 40830 382 5

Arax has stolen Aduro's soul – and now he wants Tom's...

Series 4
THE AMULET OF AVANTIA

Tom's Quest to collect the pieces of amulet from the
deadly Ghost Beasts is the only way to save his father...

978 1 40830 376 4

978 1 40830 377 1

978 1 40830 378 8

978 1 40830 379 5

978 1 40830 381 8

978 1 40830 380 1

All priced at £4.99
Vedra & Krimon: Twin Beasts of Avantia, Spiros the Ghost Phoenix and *Arax the Soul Stealer* are priced at £5.99

The Beast Quest books are available from all good
bookshops, or can be ordered direct from the publisher:
Orchard Books, PO BOX 29, Douglas IM99 1BQ.
Credit card orders please telephone 01624 836000
or fax 01624 837033 or visit our website: www.orchardbooks.co.uk
or e-mail: bookshop@enterprise.net for details.

To order please quote title, author
and ISBN and your full name and address.
Cheques and postal orders should be made payable to 'Bookpost plc.'
Postage and packing is FREE within the UK
(overseas customers should add £2.00 per book).

Prices and availability are subject to change.